THE STORY OF
A PLUSH BEAR

LAURA LEE HOPE

THE STORY OF A PLUSH BEAR

CHAPTER I

A SNOWBALL FIGHT

Down swirled the white flakes, blowing this way and that. It was snowing furiously in North Pole Land, and even the immense workshop of Santa Claus was almost buried in white. How the wind howled! It whistled down the chimneys, and blew the sparks about.

"Whew, how cold it is!" cried a Wax Doll, who did not have any shoes on, for she was not yet quite finished. "What makes such a breeze in here?" and she shivered as she pulled up over her legs a blanket of plush cloth from which Santa Claus and his men made Teddy Bears.

"It is cold," said a Celluloid Doll, who was lying on the work bench next to the wax toy. "Some one must have left a window open."

"Left a window open? There are three or four windows open!" gleefully shouted a fuzzy, Woolen Boy Doll. "Look at the snow blowing in! Hurray! Now we can have a snowball fight without going outside. Come on!" cried the Woolen Boy Doll to a little Flannel Pig who had just been stuffed with cotton. "Come on, have a snowball fight!"

"All right!" squealed the Flannel Pig. "I'll wash your face!"

"Oh, how cold it is! How cold it is!" sighed the Wax Doll. "Give me more covers, please, somebody! My feet are freezing! Who left the windows open?"

"Here, take this," called a big Plush Bear, tossing toward the Wax Doll a quilt he took from a bed in a playhouse that stood next to him on the work table. "This will keep you warm. I guess some of the men who work for Santa Claus must have gone off and forgotten to close the windows."

This is just what had happened. There had been a busy time in the North Pole workshop of Santa Claus that day, for it was getting near to Christmas. The little men, like elves, who built the Noah's Arks, the toy animals, the dolls, and the other playthings, had been as busy as bees.

Then, in the afternoon, just before dark, jolly old Santa Claus himself entered his shop, the windows of which were made from crystal-clear sheets of ice.

"What ho, my merry men!" cried Santa Claus, "you have been working very hard. Stop now, and have lunch, for we must work overtime to-night so that we may finish a lot of toys to be taken down to Earth. But now I will give you a little rest, though it is not five o'clock, when we usually stop."

"Hurray!" cried the merry little men.

They gladly laid down their tools and put aside the half-finished toys on which they had been working. Half-finished Dolls, Jumping Jacks that could not yet leap, Jacks in Boxes that could not yet spring out, trains of cars that could not yet run—all these were laid aside, together with toys completely made, so that the little men might rest themselves.

"Come to the lunch room and get some hot chocolate and some frosted cake," said Santa Claus, and away trooped the jolly little men. Just who had left some of the windows open no one knew. But they were open, and when the big storm came, in blew the snowflakes.

"I call this real jolly," said the big Plush Bear, who had given the Wax Doll the bed quilt to keep her feet warm. "I'd like to be out in this storm. But this is the next best thing. Hi there!" he called to the Flannel Pig, "look out where you're throwing snowballs! You nearly hit the Wax Doll."

"Oh, if he did that my complexion would be spoiled!" cried the beautiful toy, who was not, as yet, quite finished.

"I'll be careful," promised the Flannel Pig. "Don't you want to have fun in the snowball fight, Mr. Teddy Bear?"

"I am not a Teddy Bear!" roared the big plush creature. "Many people take me for one; but I am not, though I do look like a Teddy. But I am a real Plush Bear, and when I am wound up I can move my head and my paws and I can growl. Listen! I am wound up now!"

There was a whirring sound inside the Plush Bear as the clock work wheels began to turn, and soon his head moved slowly from side to side, he raised his paws and lowered them, and out of his red mouth came a growling voice saying:

"To be sure, I'll join the snowball fight!"

"Hurray!" cried the Woolen Boy Doll. "Now for some fun!" For though the Plush Bear had spoken with a growl he was not at all cross. That was just his way. He was really most jolly, though he had a very wise look on his plush face, as though always thinking of hard examples to solve and hard words to spell. But though he was wise, and growled when he talked, the Plush Bear was most delightful.

"Come on! We'll move over to one side where we shall not get any snow on the toys who don't like it," said the Plush Bear. With his warm coat, almost like fur, he loved to roll in the snow. So did the Flannel Pig and the Woolen Boy Doll. But the Wax Doll, who, as yet, had no shoes, the Celluloid Doll, who was only partly dressed, and some of the others did not like the cold.

Faster and faster the snow came down, and more and more white flakes blew in through the open windows of the shop of Santa Claus at the North Pole. The Plush Bear caught up a paw full of the white crystals from the bench, made them into a ball, and tossed them at the Flannel Pig. The Flannel Pig turned quickly and chased after the Woolen Boy Doll, crying:

"I'll wash your face! I'll wash your face!"

Then such fun as there was! The Wax Doll, covered up now so that her feet were no longer cold, and in a safe corner where no balls could hit her, watched the sport.

"I'm glad Santa Claus and his men took a little resting spell," said the Plush Bear, as he quickly stooped down to get out of the way of a snowball thrown by a Teddy Bear, almost like himself.

"Yes, if they were here we could have no fun," said the Flannel Pig.

And this was very true.

As I shall explain to you in this book, and as I have told you in other books of these "Make Believe Stories," the toys could pretend to come to life, move about, and have fun when no one was looking at them. They could talk, tell jokes and stories, as well as riddles, play games, have races and even snowball fights, as they were having one now. But the moment any one looked at them, or came into the room where they were playing, the toys settled back straight and stiff and still. They could listen to what was said, but they dared not speak, and they could take no part in life.

So it was that the toys were glad Santa Claus and his men had, for a little while, gone out of the big workshop. It was a wonderful place—this workshop of Santa Claus. There many of the toys in the world were made for the boys and girls of the Earth. And as fast as he had several boxes of toys ready, Santa Claus would hitch his eight reindeer to his sleigh, and down to Earth he would go. He would leave boxes and bags of toys at the different shops and warehouses, whence they were sent to other places where boys and girls could see them, and tell their fathers, mothers, sisters, brothers, uncles, aunts or cousins what they wanted for Christmas.

Biff! a big snowball went sailing across the room.

Bang! it struck the Plush Bear on his nose.

"Wuff! Wuff!" growled the Plush Bear, but he was not at all cross, and, an instant later, he sent another ball sailing toward the Flannel Pig.

"Oh, I didn't throw that! I didn't hit you!" squealed the Flannel Pig, as he tried to dodge out of the way of the mass of snow tossed by the Plush Bear.

"Never mind," growled Mr. Bruin, as the Bear was sometimes called. "It's all in fun!"

And fun it was! At other times, when they were left alone, the toys in the workshop of Santa Claus had fun, but never before, at least in a long while, had windows been left open so that the snow blew in.

"It's almost as much fun as being out doors," said the Plush Bear again, as he moved his paws and shook his head from side to side. "I only wish the Nodding Donkey could be here to enjoy it," he went on.

"Who is the Nodding Donkey?" asked the Wax Doll, as the Flannel Pig and the others stopped snowballing for a moment.

"He was a toy who was born here, and who lived here for some time, before he was taken down to Earth," answered the Plush Bear. "He could nod his head, and he did not have to be wound up with a key as I have to be. I liked the Nodding Donkey very much. But he and the China Cat have both gone away.

"However, I suppose that is the way of things up here. We are made to give happiness to boys and girls, and the only way in which we can do that is to allow ourselves to be taken to Earth by Santa Claus. Yes, I suppose I shall be taken down some day," and once more he moved his head from side to side, and looked very wise indeed, did the Plush Bear.

As I have said, he was not a Teddy Bear, though sometimes he looked like one. He was made entirely of soft, brown, silky plush. This plush covered from view the clock wheels and springs inside the Bear, which when wound up, caused him to move and growl. But the wheels did not give the Bear his wise look. That was put on his face by one of the workmen of Santa Claus.

"Oh, I know what we can do!" suddenly cried a Polar Bear, who had just shuffled along to join the fun. The Polar Bear was like the Plush Bear only a different color, the Plush Bear being brown, and the Polar Bear white.

"What shall we do?" asked the Flannel Pig, as he wiped some snow water out of one of his eyes.

"Let's build a big snow house, such as the Eskimos all about the North Pole build," went on the Polar Bear. "There is enough snow being blown in through the open windows to make a lot of houses. And we can make a hill, and slide down that, too!"

"Yes, let's do it," said the Woolen Doll Boy. But just then the Plush Bear shook his head and growled out:

"Be careful, everybody! I think some one is coming! We must not be seen in motion, or be heard talking. Keep quiet, every one!"

Each of the toys became as still as a little chocolate mouse.

Then one of the open windows was darkened as a strange creature looked in. It seemed to be a boy, but he was covered with skins and fur, almost like an animal. Only his face could be seen. His hands, as he rested them on the sill of the window, were covered with big, fur mittens.

"Oh, ho! Nobody is here! I can take one of the toys!" said the fur-dressed Eskimo boy, for such he was. "Now is my chance! I'll take that big bear!"

The Eskimo boy, one of a strange, unknown race that live at the North Pole, was just climbing in through the open window, when suddenly, at the far end of the shop, a voice cried:

"Oh, my goodness! Look what has happened! Some one left the windows open and a lot of snow has blown in! Quick, my merry men! Close the windows and start work to finish the toys! I hope none is spoiled!"

And with that Santa Claus himself hurried into the shop.

CHAPTER II

THE LITTLE ESKIMO

Following Santa Claus, his little men hurried into the North Pole shop. They were dancing and capering about, for they felt very lively after their rest, and they were ready to start again making toys, or finishing those half completed.

"Oh! Oh! Oh! Such a lot of trouble!" cried Santa Claus, but even this trouble could not keep the laughter out of his jolly voice. "Snow! Snow! Snow all over everything!" went on Saint Nicholas. "Who left the windows open so that all the flakes blew in?" he asked.

"I—I guess I did, Santa Claus," replied one of the little men who wore a red cap. "I wanted some fresh air, for I was working over the paint pots, putting blue eyes in wax dolls, and the paint smell almost choked me. So I opened some windows."

"I guess no great harm is done," said Santa Claus, looking about. "It is so cold the snow hasn't melted, and it is only melted snow that spoils toys. But I don't see how the snow got all over the floor, as well as on the benches," he added.

Ah, if Santa Claus had only seen the toys at play, throwing snowballs all about, and washing the faces of one another, he would have known how it happened. But even Santa Claus was not allowed to see the toys come to life and play.

"Get brooms, sweep up the snow, and close the windows," called Saint Nicholas. "Get the shop ready to work in again, for we are going to be very busy. The Earth children want many toys this year, and we have not made nearly enough. Clean out the snow!"

With brooms, shovels, and brushes, the merry little men fell to work, and soon the shop of Santa Claus was as it should be, and as it had been before the storm. The windows, made of sheets of ice, were pulled down, and soon there was the hum of songs all through the shop, for the men of Santa Claus sang as they worked.

One of the men, as he pulled down the window near his bench, where he was making a lot of little animals for a Noah's Ark, looked out through the pane of ice glass.

"What do you see?" asked the workman next him.

"Oh, one of those odd Eskimo children, all dressed in fur, was right under this window," answered the other little man. "He must have been here when the windows were open. Maybe he wanted to see us making toys. Well, he won't see any better toy than the Plush Bear I just finished," said the little man proudly.

"No, indeed!" agreed the second little man. "But does Santa Claus know about these little Eskimo children coming around his workshop?" he asked.

"Oh, they never bother us," was the answer. "Now we mustn't talk any more, for we have many toys to make for the Earth children."

So the little men became very busy—too busy to talk, though the Plush Bear heard them singing as they made toy after toy. The Plush Bear and the other playthings could hear what was said, though they could take no part in the talk while Santa Claus, or any of his men, were in the shop. And Santa Claus was there now, seeing that each one of his tiny elves made as many toys as possible.

"Well, we certainly had a good time for a while!" thought the Plush Bear to himself. "What fun that snowball fight was! I'd like another. I didn't feel a bit cold!"

And no wonder. His coat of silk plush was as warm as the fur coat of a real bear. The Plush toy was looking straight at the Polar Bear and the big, white fellow seemed to be blinking his eyes at the other Bear.

All through the great North Pole workshop of Santa Claus the little men were busy, singing over their tasks. But they could not work all night and all day as well, so at last there came an hour when Santa Claus rang a bell and said:

"Now, my merry men, it is time for you to go to bed. Be up early in the morning to make more toys. Good-night, everybody!"

With that he went out, buttoning his fur coat about him, and the workmen, after putting away their tools, followed. Santa Claus and his men slept in snow castles not far from the workshop.

It was almost dark in the toy shop now. Outside the Northern Lights glowed faintly, and inside only a little candle was left gleaming, its beams reflected in some shiny gold stars that were to go on the tops of Christmas trees later on.

"Be Careful, Everybody!" Said the Plush Bear.

"Hello, everybody!" softly called the voice of the Flannel Pig, as he peered out from the roof of a toy dog house, where he had been put by one of the workmen. "Now we can have some more fun!"

"We must be sure every one is gone," said the Plush Bear, as he began to swing his head from side to side. For he had been wound up, and now the wheels and springs inside him were beginning to move.

"Oh, every one is gone," said the Wax Doll. "And this time they will stay away all night. Now we can have our usual fun."

"Is there any snow left?" asked the Polar Bear. "I should like to wash the face of the Plush Bear."

"And I'd wash yours, too!" laughed the Plush Bear. "But the little men swept out all the snow and closed the windows. There isn't so much as an icicle left."

"Too bad!" sighed the Polar Bear. "Well, we'll have fun some other way. Let's see, what shall we do? Have any of you ever seen me turn somersaults?" he asked, after a moment's pause.

"No. Can you do it?" asked the Plush Bear.

"You should see me!" boasted the big white Bear. "I don't believe anywhere in North Pole Land you will find a better somersault turner than I. Watch me!"

The Plush Bear and the other toys leaned forward from the shelves and tables where they sat or stood to see what would happen. If they had not been so eager to see what the Polar Bear was going to do some of them might have noticed a small, dark figure stealing up outside the workshop of Santa Claus, and stopping beneath one of the ice windows.

This little figure was that of an Eskimo boy—the same little chap, all dressed in sealskin and fur, who had looked in and almost reached through the window to take out the Plush Bear when he had interrupted the toys in the midst of their snowball fight.

"Ah, now is my chance!" murmured the little Eskimo boy, as he stepped softly over the snow, coming nearer and nearer to the workshop of Santa Claus. "If I can open a window I'll take out that Plush Bear, cart him off to the igloo, and have a lot of fun."

The Eskimo boy lived with his father and mother in a house made of blocks of snow and ice. This house was called an "igloo," and it takes its name from the house built by the seals in the far North. The Eskimos build their houses the same shape as the houses made in the ice by the seals. If you cut an orange or an apple in half, and put the flat side down on a table, you will see exactly how an Eskimo igloo is shaped.

"Oh, if I can only get the Plush Bear!" thought the Eskimo boy, as he stepped softly nearer and nearer to the workshop of Santa Claus.

It was not very dark in North Pole Land just then. Though the sun had gone down, and the long winter had set in, still there were the Northern Lights, which glowed and flickered in the sky and made enough of a gleam for the Eskimo boy to see his way over the snow. The snow, too, helped to make it less dark.

Ever since he had seen the Plush Bear through the window of Santa Claus' workshop that day, the Eskimo boy had wanted the plaything. So after his supper of seal fat and blubber, with a piece of tallow candle, which was to him what candy is to you, the boy, well wrapped in fur, started out from his igloo.

All this while, or at least after Santa Claus and his men had gone, the Plush Bear and the other toys were having fun among themselves. As I have told you, the Polar Bear was getting ready to turn somersaults to amuse the other toys.

"Watch me now!" cried the Polar Bear, as he leaned over and got ready to stand on his head.

"Say, why don't you turn some somersaults?" the Flannel Pig asked of the Plush Bear.

"Maybe I will after he gets through," the Plush Bear answered.

The Eskimo boy was now at one of the windows of the shop—a window which had for a pane a clear sheet of ice. The Eskimo boy blew his warm breath on this window pane, close to the place where, inside, there was a catch to hold the window shut.

"Hoo! Hoo! Hoo!" breathed the Eskimo boy on the glass. And his breath was warm, just as yours is when you melt the frost on your window glass at home. Very soon the fur-clad boy had melted a hole in the ice pane. After that it was easy for him to slip his hand in and turn back the window catch.

The Eskimo boy did not know it was wrong thus to take a toy from the workshop of Santa Claus. He only knew that he wanted the Plush Bear, and that this was the easiest way to get it.

Softly he raised the window, after he had turned back the catch. There, in front of him on one of the tables, stood the Plush Bear and many other Christmas toys. But the Eskimo boy had eyes only for the Plush Bear.

"What fun I shall have with you!" whispered the Eskimo boy. He reached forth his hand and took the wonderful plaything.

Just at this time the Polar Bear was turning a somersault, and the eyes of all the other toys were looking at him.

If they had not been looking at the Polar Bear they would have seen the Eskimo boy open the window. And had he once looked at the toys they would have had to stop talking and moving. But, as it happened, none of the toys saw him.

The Plush Bear had just been going to clap his paws together to applaud the Polar Bear's trick of turning a somersault, when the Plush Bear felt himself lifted up.

"Oh!" he said faintly, and then he saw that he must not move or speak, for the Eskimo boy was looking straight at him.

"Ha, now I have you, Mr. Plush Bear," whispered the Eskimo boy, and he quickly drew his arm back out of the open window, taking the wonderful toy with him. He slipped the Plush Bear under his coat of fur, and away he sped over the snow, sparkling in the Northern Lights. Over the snow ran the Eskimo boy, taking to his igloo the Plush Bear.

"Oh, dear me," thought the Plush Bear, "this is a strange adventure, indeed! I hoped I might go to Earth in the sleigh of Santa Claus, as the Nodding Donkey did, but now, it seems, I must stay at the North Pole in a snow and ice hut! Oh, dear! What is going to happen to me?"

CHAPTER III

OUT ALL NIGHT

"There! What do you think of that for a somersault?" cried the Polar Bear, as he flopped over on his back. "Can you do as well as that, Mr. Plush Bear?"

"Oh, what a wonderful fellow the Polar Bear is!" cried the Wax Doll, who now had on her shoes so she could walk about on the broad workshop bench. "Quite remarkable!"

"The Plush Bear can do as well!" squealed the Flannel Pig, making his nose wrinkle up in a funny way. "Come on, Plush Bear!" he cried. "Show them how you turn somersaults!"

This talk took place just after the Polar Bear had done his trick, and right after the Eskimo boy had opened the window and taken away the toy he so much wanted.

None of the toys, except the Plush Bear, had seen the Eskimo boy, and the boy had not looked at any of the other toys, so they did not have to stop what they were doing. And as the Eskimo boy popped his hand out of the window, almost as soon as he had popped it in, the toys kept right on with what they were doing.

"Come, let's see you turn a somersault, Plush Bear!" called the Polar Bear to his friend.

"Yes! Yes!" cried the other playthings! "Let's have a somersault race!"

They turned toward that part of the work bench where they thought the Plush Bear would be standing, but the Plush Bear was not there.

"Oh, he's gone!" squealed the Flannel Pig.

"Maybe he got down on the floor to practice a somersault, so he can beat me! But he'll have hard work!" growled the Polar Bear. But he was not cross when he growled. It was just his way of speaking, as it was also that of the Plush Bear.

"No, he isn't on the floor!" said the Wax Doll, leaning over the edge of the table to look down.

"Oh, he has fallen out of the window!" suddenly cried the Flannel Pig. "See, the window is open! The Plush Bear must have fallen into the snow outside."

"We must get him back!"

"Throw him a piece of a doll's clothes-line and haul him up!"

"Get a ladder from one of the toy fire engines!"

13

"Let's all go down after him! Maybe he bumped his nose!"

These were only a few of the shouts and cries that came when it was discovered that the window was open and that the Plush Bear was gone.

The Eskimo boy had not stopped to close the window after opening it to take the toy he so much wanted. And now the toys, crowding on the sill, which was close to the work bench, looked out in the snow under the window. It was light enough for them to see quite well.

"Come on back here, Plush Bear!" called the Flannel Pig, who was quite friendly with the big toy. "I want to see you turn a somersault."

"Yes, come on back, unless you're afraid that I can beat you!" growled the Polar Bear.

"Maybe he is afraid, and ran away," suggested the Wax Doll, who seemed more friendly to the Polar Bear.

"No, indeed!" squealed the Flannel Pig. "The Plush Bear is a brave fellow, and he is very wise! He would not run away. The window must have come open and he tumbled out."

"But he isn't down there in the snow," said a toy Fireman, looking carefully below. "If he was down there I could fix a ladder for him so he could climb up. But he isn't there."

"Where can he be?" asked the Flannel Pig. "He was standing near me one minute, saying how he was going to turn a somersault, and when next I looked he was gone."

"See! There are footprints in the snow under the window," said the Polar Bear, who had come to the sill. "Maybe Santa Claus or some of his men came along outside, and took the Plush Bear away."

"They would not do that," declared the Wax Doll. "Santa Claus would not take just one of us toys. When he takes any, he takes a whole sleigh-load to Earth for the children. No, there is something strange about this!"

And indeed there was, as we know. The Eskimo boy had the Plush Bear, but the toys knew nothing of this. However, there was nothing they could do.

After calling softly to the Plush Bear to come back, but receiving no answer, about a dozen of the Jumping Jacks, by climbing up and all pulling together on the window, managed to close it to keep out the cold, night air.

"Well, since there is no one else to turn somersaults with me, I'll do it alone," said the Polar Bear. So he flipped and flopped over again, and the other toys played games among themselves, but the nice Plush Bear was not among them.

He was under the fur coat of the Eskimo boy, being carried across the snow to the ice hut, or igloo. The door to this igloo was not like the door to your home. It was just a hole, with some pieces of fur and skin hung over it to keep out the cold wind. Ski, which was the name of the Eskimo boy, pushed aside this curtain of fur as he crawled into the igloo, with the Plush Bear beneath his warm jacket. The doorway, or hole, was made small to keep out as much cold as possible, and Ski had to stoop down and crawl on his hands and knees to get in.

Inside the igloo there were no tables and chairs, such as there are in your house. There were just some slabs of ice set here and there, being raised a little from the icy floor. On the floor were skins to make it as warm as possible, and in the middle of the igloo was a sort of lamp, or stove, made of stone, filled with oil in which floated a wick that was burning. This lamp-stove was all the Eskimos had to heat and cook with. But as they wore their fur clothes all winter long, never taking them off, they did not catch cold.

"Look!" said Ski, the Eskimo boy, as he pulled the Plush Bear out from under his fur coat and set the toy down on a shelf of ice in the igloo, where the rays from the oil lamp fell upon it. "See what I have!" and his father and mother and his brothers and sisters leaned forward to look at the strange object.

There was not much room in the igloo, and the Eskimo family was rather crowded. But they did not mind this, as it was much warmer than if they had lived in a big room. In fact, except in the center, one could not stand up in the igloo. The roof was too low.

"Where did you get that?" asked Ski's father, as he looked at the Plush Bear.

"He was in the big igloo, far over the snow, near the big ice mountain," answered the Eskimo boy. "I saw him through a window, and I wanted him. When all in the igloo were asleep I breathed on the ice pane, opened the window, and took this Bear. Now he is mine!"

"Yes, I know that big igloo," said Ski's father. "There was none like it where we came from. I do not know what it is."

Ski's family had just moved to North Pole Land, and they had never heard of Santa Claus, though the other Eskimos of this country were well acquainted with Saint Nicholas. To Ski and his family the workshop of Santa Claus was just a big "igloo."

"Is not this Bear nice?" asked Ski, of his brothers and sisters.

"But he is not like the bears here," said Kiki, one of the Eskimo girls. "He is brown, like the seals. The North Bears are white."

"There was a white Bear in the big igloo, but I would rather have this one," said Ski. "I will always keep him."

During this time the Plush Bear, of course, had not dared to say a word or move by himself. He was being watched too closely. But he could hear what was said, and he wondered what was going to happen to him.

"I shall be dreadfully lonesome if I have to stay here," thought the Plush Bear. "There is not another toy in the whole place!"

There was another toy, but the Plush Bear did not know it. This toy was a rudely carved Wooden Doll, owned by Kiki. She had wrapped this Wooden Doll in a bit of sealskin and put it in her bed to keep it warm. For to Kiki the piece of wood, which looked something like a Doll, was as much alive as your Doll is to you girls.

"That is a wonderful thing, Ski," said the Eskimo boy's father. "Never have I seen such a thing in all my life!"

Ski's father leaned forward and touched the Plush Bear. And he happened to touch the very spring that set the toy animal in motion. For the Plush Bear was all wound up when Ski reached through the window and took him, and all that was needed was a touch to send him off.

Immediately the Plush Bear began to move his head from side to side, growls came out of his red mouth, and his paws waved to and fro. He behaved almost like a small, live bear.

"Wow!" cried Ski, leaping back when he saw the Plush Bear beginning to move.

"Wow!" cried Ski's father, mother and sisters and brothers, and they, too, leaped back.

"Gurr-r-r-r! Gurr-r-r-r!" growled the Plush Bear, and he moved his paws and head faster than ever. He was not doing this himself, you understand. He was not making believe come to life. He was only doing as all the other spring toys do—moving when the wheels within him moved.

"Wow!" cried Ski's father again. "This is magic! This bear is bewitched! It will bring us bad luck! It must not stay in my igloo!"

"Oh, please let me keep it!" begged Ski, as his father caught up the Plush Bear.

"No! No! It would be dangerous! It would bring us bad luck! There is a witch in that bear!" murmured Ski's mother.

"Never have I seen such a thing!" went on Ski's father in awe and wonder. "We must not keep it! If we allowed it to stay in this igloo we should freeze, I should never catch any seals, and our blubber fat would become so hard we could not eat it. I must take this magic bear that moves back to the big igloo!"

So, though Ski begged his father to be allowed to keep the toy, the Eskimo man thrust the bear under his fur coat and crawled out of the igloo into the glow of the Northern Lights.

"I must take it back to the big igloo," murmured Ski's father. "Then will the bad magic pass away."

You see he did not know, never having seen such a toy before, and never having heard of machinery—Ski's father did not know what a delightful toy the Plush Bear was. All he thought of was bad luck and magic.

Quickly Ski's father hitched his team of dogs to the long, low wooden sled.

Crack! went the long whip over their heads, but the Eskimo man did not let the lash fall on the animals.

Over the snow and ice they drew the sled, on which Ski's father sat well wrapped in fur blankets. Nearer they came to the workshop of Santa Claus—the "big igloo" as Ski had called it.

"I will leave the magic bear that moves beneath one of the windows," murmured Ski's father. "Then will the bad luck pass from us."

He guided his dog team up under the very window out of which Ski had taken the bear, for the man could see Ski's footprints in the snow.

"There! Now I am done with you!" whispered Ski's father, as he dropped the Plush Bear in the snow and turned his dog team around to go back to his igloo.

As for the Plush Bear, his head moved, he growled, and his paws waved to and fro as long as the spring was wound up. But when it ran down, as it did in a little while, he was motionless. Except that now, as no one could see him, he was allowed to make believe come to life and could do as he pleased.

"Well, this is certainly a fine state of affairs!" said the Plush Bear to himself, speaking out loud, as there were no human ears to hear. "Taken away to an ice house, scaring an Eskimo family half to death, and then to be brought back here and dumped in a snow bank! It's a good thing I have on a warm plush coat, or I'd surely freeze! I wonder if I can get back into the shop?"

But this the Bear could not do. The window had been pulled down and shut by the Jumping Jacks, and the hole Ski had breathed in the icy pane was too small for the Plush Bear to crawl through, even if he could have reached it. He tried to call out, to make the toys inside hear him, so they might rescue him, but they had gone to sleep after their evening of fun.

So the Plush Bear had to stay out in the snow bank near the workshop of Santa Claus all night. It was cold and dreary, but he made the best of it.

"When morning comes they will take me in," he thought. "The night can not last forever."

CHAPTER IV

IN THE TOY SHOP

Slowly the night passed. Well it was for the Plush Bear that he was warmly clad in such a warm coat, or he might have been frozen stiff. As it was, his wheels and springs had to be oiled several times after his long night spent in a snowdrift.

In the morning Santa Claus and his men hurried into the workshop after breakfast. There was a hum and a bustle, whistling and singing, and the sound of many tools being used.

"Lively, my merry men, lively!" cried Santa Claus, with a laugh, as he passed from bench to bench. "I will soon make a trip to Earth, and I shall need many toys to take with me. I want a big bagful to load into my sleigh. My reindeer are waiting. All I need is toys—more toys—all the toys you can make!"

"You shall have them, Santa Claus! You shall have them!" cried the merry little men, and they began to work as fast as they could.

At one of the benches Santa Claus observed a little man looking about as though in search of something. The little man moved his tools to one side, he shifted toys here and there, and then he looked under his bench.

"What are you looking for?" asked Santa Claus, as he passed up and down the aisles.

"Why, yesterday, I finished a fine Plush Bear," answered the workman. "I set it over here, but now it is gone. You did not take it to Earth, did you?"

"Oh, no," answered Santa Claus. "I have not been to Earth for some time. But I am going soon again. Ha! I know what may have happened," he said suddenly. "The windows were open yesterday. The Plush Bear may have fallen out of the window!"

It did not take the workman more than an instant to raise the sash and poke out his head. He looked down into the bank of snow under the window.

"Here he is!" he cried. "Just as you thought, Santa Claus, the Plush Bear fell out of the window! He isn't hurt a bit! I'll get him back again. Ho! Ho! My Plush Bear fell out of the window!"

Of course this didn't happen at all, but it was the only way Santa Claus and his men could think of the accident having happened. But we know about the little Eskimo boy, and how his father left the Plush Bear in the snow bank.

"There you are!" said the toy workman as he came in with the Plush Bear and set him on the bench again. "I'm glad to get you back. Only for your warm coat you might have frozen. I must see if you work all right."

But the cold had chilled the wheels and springs inside the Plush Bear, and it was not until after some warm oil had been poured on them that they worked properly again. Then, when the Plush Bear was wound up, he could growl, wag his head, and wave his paws as well as ever.

"Once more you are ready to go down to Earth, as soon as Santa Claus is ready to take you," said the workman, as he started to make a toy fire engine that, some day, would gladden the heart of a lucky boy.

As for the other toys in Santa Claus' shop, they had been very much surprised to see the Plush Bear brought back into their midst again. But while Saint Nicholas and his helpers were around, nothing could be said, no questions could be asked, and Plush Bear could tell none of his adventures.

But when night came again, and the Northern Lights glowed, when the janitor had mended the hole in the ice pane, breathed on by the Eskimo boy, when all was still and quiet, the Flannel Pig leaned over toward the Plush Bear and whispered:

"Where were you? What happened? Did you try to run away?"

"Indeed I did not run away! Some one ran away with me! An Eskimo boy, and he took me to his igloo, but his father would not let him keep me because he thought I was magic and would bring him bad luck," answered the Plush Bear.

"My, what marvelous adventures!" exclaimed the Wax Doll, who was fond of using big words. "Please tell us all about it."

"Yes, do," growled the Polar Bear. "And after that we can have a somersault race. You missed it last night. We thought you had fallen out of the window."

"I'll tell you of my adventures," said the Plush Bear, and he did, from the time Ski took him away until the workman found him in the snow bank.

"I told you his adventures would be marvelous," said the Wax Doll. "Nothing as strange will happen to you when you are taken to Earth, Mr. Plush Bear."

But just wait and see. You never can tell what is going to happen, and the Plush Bear may have even more strange adventures.

That night in the shop of Santa Claus passed all too soon for the Plush Bear. When he had finished telling his story the Flannel Pig cried:

"Let's have a game of tag!"

"All right! I'll be it!" agreed a Jumping Jack, and he was such a lively fellow that in less than a second he had tagged an Elephant. The Elephant was so large and such a slow chap that he was it for a long time. He could hardly tag any one, not even the Plush Bear and the Polar Bear, who, also being large animal toys, had to move slowly. But they were not as slow as the Elephant.

"Oh, this is no fun!" said the Elephant after a while. "I can't catch any of you! Let's play hide and go seek! I'll have some chance in that game!"

So they played that, and told stories and sang songs until it was almost morning, and time for Santa Claus and his men to open the shop again. Then the toys became quiet, as usual.

That day Saint Nicholas walked up and down among the benches and spoke to his workmen.

"I will go to Earth to-morrow," said Santa Claus. "Get ready all the toys you can, and I will fill my sleigh. I will load it to-night."

And the toys who heard this were very much excited, wondering who would be taken and who would be left.

"I'll take this Plush Bear!" said Santa Claus that evening, as he began selecting the toys he wanted for his sack to take to Earth. "And I'll take the Wax Doll, the Flannel Pig, and the Elephant. I want a lot of other dolls, plenty of drums, some Jumping Jacks, some Jacks in the Box, some toy soldiers, some toy engines, trains of cars, toy guns and enough more to fill my sack to running over. It is so near Christmas that I need all the toys I can pile into my sleigh."

The Plush Bear was lifted off the bench by one of the workmen and put in a box, after being wrapped in tissue paper.

"I hope they don't smother me!" thought the Bear, but he need not have been afraid. His last glimpse was of the Wax Doll. She, too, was well wrapped and placed in a box so her complexion would not be spoiled.

"I did hope I'd have a chance to bid farewell to the toys that are left," thought the Plush Bear, as he was placed in the sleigh of Santa Claus. "But some of them are coming with me, that's a comfort. We shall not have room to move around, though, and hardly a chance to talk on our trip to the Earth. However, I suppose it cannot be helped. This is part of our adventures in life."

A little later there was a merry jingle of bells, and Santa Claus could be heard calling:

"Hi, Prancer! Steady there, Dashaway! Wait a minute, Comet!"

"Those are the reindeer," whispered the Wax Doll, through the side of her box to the Plush Bear in his box.

"I supposed so," was the answer. "I hope I am not made seasick on this voyage through the air."

"Seasick! The idea! The sleigh of Santa Claus is not a boat!" squealed the Flannel Pig.

Then the sack of toys was lifted up and put in the sleigh. The reindeer shook their heads, making the bells jingle more merrily than ever. There came a jolly laugh from Santa Claus, and then he cried:

"Away we go! Over the ice! Over the snow! Down to the Earth below!"

And a moment later the Plush Bear and the other toys found themselves being swiftly carried through the cold air. But they were snug and warm in the sleigh of Santa Claus.

Of all the things that happened to the Plush Bear and the other toys on their trip from the shop of Santa Claus to Earth I have not room to tell you here. Enough to say that, unlike the Nodding Donkey, they suffered no accident. None of them was tossed out into a drift of snow. Then, finally, the big sack of toys was left at one of the many big buildings on Earth, whence they were to be divided among the toy shops.

And one day, after having been cooped up in his box for a long time, so, at least, it seemed to him, the Plush Bear's eyes were suddenly dazzled by a flash of light.

"I wonder if I am back at the North Pole," he thought. "Has that Eskimo boy caught me again, and is he taking me to his igloo? Are these Northern Lights that flash in front of me?"

But they were not, though they came from the same cause—electricity. The glare that dazzled the eyes of the Plush Bear came from the electric lights of a large store, where he was being unpacked, together with other toys. There was a rustle of paper as the Plush Bear was unwrapped, and then a voice cried:

"Oh, Father, see what a fine toy! And it's the kind you wind up! Oh, I shall love this Plush Bear!"

"Do not squeeze him too tightly, Angelina," said a white-haired and white-whiskered old man, who was helping two women lift the toys out of the big box in which they had come. "You may break some of the wheels or springs."

"Oh, I shan't hug him too tightly," said Angelina, laughing. "But he is certainly a lovely Plush Bear."

"Yes, he is very nice," said the old gentleman. "What have you, Geraldine?" he asked his other daughter.

"An Elephant," was the answer. "But he doesn't wind up. However, he will look well in the window."

"Yes," said the old man, "to-morrow we will decorate the show windows for the Christmas trade. The Plush Bear must surely stand in the window. Some one will see him and buy him."

"Well, at last I seem to have reached a toy shop—the very place I most wanted to come to," thought the Plush Bear. "I wonder who the old gentleman is?"

Had the Plush Bear been able to read he would have seen in white letters on one of the windows the name:

HORATIO MUGG

TOY DEALER

But the Plush Bear did not need this to tell him he was in the very place he wished to be.

"Now some girl or boy will buy me, I hope, and I shall have more adventures," thought the new toy.

The Plush Bear, who was taken from his box by Angelina, one of Mr. Mugg's daughters, was placed safely on a shelf, and the unpacking of the toys went on. It was evening, and the store was closed for the day. But Mr. Mugg took this time to open his new shipment of Christmas goods.

Geraldine had just lifted out the Wax Doll, and the Plush Bear was wondering when he would have a chance to talk to her and his other friends from the shop of Santa Claus when, all of a sudden, from the rear of the toy store, which was in darkness, came a strange sound.

There was a banging, slamming noise, then several bumps, and finally a loud whistle.

"Goodness; what's that?" exclaimed Angelina.

"I hope that isn't a policeman whistling, to tell us there is another fire!" said Geraldine.

"Or that burglars are trying to break in to take the new toys," added her sister.

They looked at their father, who laid down a Noah's Ark he was just looking at and started toward the back of the store. As he did so the noise became louder; bumping, banging, crashing, and above it all sounded the shrill toot-toot of whistles.

"Dear me, what is happening?" thought the Plush Bear.

Horatio Mugg, owner of the toy store where the Plush Bear was now at home, hurried to the back of the shop. It was here that the noise had come from, and the sound was still keeping up as Mr. Mugg turned on an electric light.

Then the Plush Bear, who was listening as closely as were Geraldine and Angelina, heard Mr. Mugg laugh, and with that the rattling, banging and tooting noise came to a stop.

"Ha! Ha! Ha!" laughed Mr. Mugg again.

"What is it?" asked Angelina. "It isn't a burglar, evidently."

"Nor a policeman nor a fire," Geraldine added.

"None of them," answered Mr. Mugg. "One of the toy trains of cars that I wound up this evening just started off by itself. I guess some of the toys must have wanted a ride, and the Engineer of the toy train tooted his whistle to tell them to get aboard."

"Why, Father!" exclaimed Geraldine, "the toys couldn't want a ride. They can't do anything like that."

"Well, I wouldn't be so sure," said Mr. Mugg, as his two daughters entered the rear room to see what had caused all the racket. "Sometimes I feel that these toys know more than we think they do," he went on. "Take that new Plush Bear," he added, pointing to the other room where Bruin was sitting on a shelf. "See how wise he looks? He seems about to speak. And if he ever should come to life I think he would enjoy a ride in a toy train."

"Oh, but he can't come to life!" exclaimed Angelina.

"Ha! can't I, though?" whispered the Plush Bear to himself. "You just ought to see us toys after dark! No, on second thought, it is just as well you don't see us," he went on. "For if you looked at us we couldn't say a word or move about. It is best that you do not know we can pretend to be alive."

Angelina and Geraldine looked at the toy train which had caused the excitement. It was a new engine and cars that had been unpacked that evening by their father. Mr. Mugg had wound up the spring in the engine, which was very much like a real one, with a bell, whistle, and even an iron Engineer in the cab. The toy train, all wound up and ready to go, had been left on the floor in a rear room. Then, when Mr. Mugg and his daughters were unpacking the Plush Bear and other toys, the little train, in some manner, had started off by itself, had run along the floor, banging into the walls, bumping over other toys, and with the whistle going:

Toot! Toot! Toot!

"What started it?" asked Angelina, when the train had been put in a safe place.

"Oh, I think the spring began to unwind of itself," answered Mr. Mugg. "Or our walking around may have jarred the engine, and started it off. At any rate no harm is done, and now we must finish unpacking the toys."

The toy-dealer and his two daughters were soon busy over the large packing box, and the Plush Bear and his friends from the workshop of Santa Claus looked on, well pleased to be out of the box.

"This is ever so much a nicer place than the igloo of Ski, the Eskimo boy," thought the Plush Bear. "I would not want to be up in that bleak North Pole Land, unless I were with Santa Claus, and of course one cannot stay long in his workshop. I think I shall have much more fun here. There is so much light and happiness."

It was nearly midnight when Mr. Mugg and his daughters finished unpacking the toys. All about the floor wrapping paper and the covers of boxes were scattered. The toys, as they were taken out of the case, had been set on shelves about the room.

"This will be enough for to-night," said the toy-dealer after a while. "We will leave things as they are, now that we have all the toys unpacked. To-morrow I will put some in the show window, and the boys and girls will come to buy them."

"Be sure and put the Plush Bear in the window," said Angelina. "I know he'll be one of the first to go, he is so cute and he can do so many things when he is wound up. He shakes his head and moves his paws."

"He is a good toy," said Mr. Mugg. And a little later the toy shop was in darkness, except for one light that was left burning all night.

"Oh, ho!" thought the Plush Bear, when he saw Mr. Mugg and his daughters leave. "Now is our chance! Now we can come to life!"

He turned his head to one side, and spoke to the Wax Doll.

"How do you like it here?" asked the Plush Bear.

"Oh, very much," the Doll answered. "As soon as we get to know the other toys I'm sure we shall like it."

"We are glad to welcome you here," said a Jumping Jack, who had been in Mr. Mugg's store for a long time. "Make yourselves at home. After a bit we shall have some fun. You just came from North Pole Land, didn't you?"

"Yes," answered the Plush Bear. "But we like it here very much. Come, Miss Wax Doll," he went on, "allow me the pleasure of taking you for a walk through the shop."

The Wax Doll and the Plush Bear got down off the shelf where they had been put, and began to move about. Some of the other new toys did the same, while about them crowded the playthings that had been on the shelves and the counters for some days.

"Take a look through the store," suggested the older Jumping Jack to the Plush Bear, "and then come back and we'll have some fun."

The Plush Bear and the Wax Doll, who took hold of his paw, moved along through the different rooms of the toy store. Everywhere they went they were made welcome by the playthings that had been in stock for some time. The old toys were glad to welcome the new ones.

Suddenly the Plush Bear and the Wax Doll found themselves in a strange place. All about were shining tools, pots of glue, pieces of wood, strips of cloth, glass eyes, wooden arms and legs, odd ears, noses, tails and heads.

"Oh, what a queer place!" cried the Wax Doll. "I don't like it here! What is it?"

"I hardly know," answered the Plush Bear.

"This is the repair department," said the Jumping Jack, who had followed the two new toys. "It is here that Mr. Mugg mends the toys that get broken in the store, or toys that get broken when the boys and girls play with them. We had a fire here, not long ago, and the place is rather upset, but don't mind that. It is almost in order again, but there are always things scattered about in this repair department. If ever you lose an eye or an ear, Mr. Plush Bear, just come in here and Mr. Mugg will make you a new one," said the Jumping Jack.

"That's a comfort," answered the Plush Bear, laughing. "So you have had a fire here? I thought the place smelled rather smoky."

"It's just the way I smelled after I climbed up the string, too near the gas jet, and burned my trousers," said a voice that seemed to come from one of the shelves in the repair room.

"Who is that?" whispered the Wax Doll.

"The Calico Clown," answered the Jumping Jack. "He came here to have a new cap put on him."

"That's right," said the Clown, and he made a polite bow to the Plush Bear and the Wax Doll. "Sidney, the boy who owns me, was playing circus with me. His brother, who owns the Monkey on a Stick, was trying to make me jump over the Monkey, when my cap caught on the stick and was ripped off. So they brought me here to have Mr. Mugg make me a new one. But did you hear about how I burned my trousers?" asked the Calico Clown.

"I never did, having just arrived here," said the Plush Bear.

"Oh, you should hear that story!" cried the Clown. "It was quite funny in a way, though I did not think so at the time. In fact, there has been a book made about it, and about some of my other adventures. I must tell you of them."

"I should be delighted to hear them," said the Wax Doll, who seemed to have taken quite a liking to the Calico Clown.

"Baa! Baa!" suddenly called a voice from another shelf. "I have had adventures also. After you finish telling about how you burned your trousers, Mr. Clown, I'll tell how I was once down in a coal hole."

"Who is that?" asked the Plush Bear in a low tone of the Jumping Jack.

"That is a Lamb on Wheels," was the answer. "How comes it that you are here, Miss Lamb?" the Jack answered. "I didn't hear that you had had an accident."

"Oh, yes; but not a very bad one," bleated the Lamb. "One of my wheels came off when Mirabell, the little girl who owns me, let me fall. Her brother Arnold, who has a Bold Tin Soldier and his men, tried to fix me, but his father brought me here for Mr. Mugg to operate on. I shall be well again in a few days, and go back home. But who are the visitors?" asked the Lamb.

"Oh, excuse me," said the Jumping Jack. "Let me introduce Mr. Plush Bear and Miss Wax Doll from North Pole Land," and the Bear and Doll made polite bows, as did the Lamb on Wheels and the Calico Clown.

Then the toys talked together and had a good time among themselves until morning came, when they had to go back to their places and become quiet. As soon as the store was opened for business Mr. Mugg and his daughters began arranging the playthings. The Plush Bear was put in the show window, with the Wax Doll and some of the other new gifts. It was the first time in his life that he had been in such a place, and you may be sure the Plush Bear looked about him with eagerness.

He was gazing out into a busy street—a street where people were passing up and down all the while—a street in which there was a layer of newly-fallen snow, only not as much as at the North Pole.

"I wonder if Santa Claus is here?" thought the Plush Bear.

But he could not speak aloud because so many eyes—those of the passers-by in the street and the customers in the store—were watching. There was so much to see that the Plush Bear did not know at which to look first, but, all of a sudden, he heard a voice saying:

"Oh, I want that Plush Bear! I want that! Can he do any tricks?"

The Plush Bear felt himself being lifted out of the show window of the toy shop. The springs inside him were wound up by Mr. Mugg and when he was set down on a showcase near the window the Bear began to move his head and paws, and from his red mouth came a make-believe growl.

"Oh, I want him! I want him!" the eager voice went on, and the Plush Bear was caught up by a fat boy—the very fattest and jolliest boy that the toy had ever seen. "I want this Plush Bear for my very own!" cried the fat boy. "He's the best toy I ever saw!"

CHAPTER VI

OUT OF THE WINDOW

"Don't squeeze the Bear so hard, Arthur," said a lady who was with the fat boy. "You may break the toy before I have paid for him."

"The Plush Bear is strong and well-made, Mrs. Rowe," said Mr. Mugg. "He is one of the newest of the Christmas toys, and I only put him in the show window this morning."

"And I saw him when I was walking along!" exclaimed Arthur Rowe, the jolly fat boy. "As soon as I saw him I knew I'd like him! Oh, Mother, hear him growl! And see him wave his paws!"

Indeed the Plush Bear was doing all his tricks, for he had been wound up by Mr. Mugg for that very purpose. There he sat on the top of the glass showcase, growling away (make believe of course) and waving his paws like a real bear.

Other persons in the toy store crowded up to the showcase to watch the Plush Bear do his tricks, and Arthur, the jolly fat boy, laughed loud and long as his plaything amused the throng. For the Plush Bear was to belong to Arthur. Passing down the street early that Winter morning, he had seen the toy in Mr. Mugg's window, and had begged his mother to stop and go in and inquire about him.

"Wrap him up, Mr. Mugg, please," said Arthur, when the spring was all unwound and the wheels inside the Plush Bear no longer moved his paws and head and caused him to growl. "Wrap him up, and I'll take him home. I guess Dick and Arnold and Herbert and Sidney will wish they had a toy like this!"

The Plush Bear again felt himself being lifted up by Mr. Mugg, who put him in tissue paper and then in the same box in which the Bear had traveled to Earth from the shop of Santa Claus.

"Good-by, Wax Doll! Good-by, Jumping Jack, Elephant and all my friends," said the Plush Bear to himself as the tissue paper covered his eyes and shut out the sight of the other toys in the store. "Good-by! I don't know when I shall see you again!"

Of course the Plush Bear dared not say this out loud, for he was being watched. And he dared not move of his own accord for the same reason. He felt a little sad at leaving all his toy friends, but he liked the looks of the fat boy, and Arthur seemed like one who would make a kind master.

"Oh, what fun I'll have with my Plush Bear!" said the fat boy, as he walked out of the toy store with his mother. "I'll invite Dick over with his White Rocking Horse, Arnold with his Bold Tin Soldiers, Herbert with his Monkey on a Stick, and Sidney with his Calico Clown. We'll have a lot of fun!"

"I thought you said Sidney's Calico Clown was broken," remarked Mrs. Rowe as she and Arthur got into their automobile.

"Only the Clown's cap was torn off when they were playing circus the other day," said Arthur. "Mirabell's Lamb on Wheels was broken, too, and I guess they're both in Mr. Mugg's toy shop being fixed."

"Indeed they are there," thought the Plush Bear, who could hear all that was said through the tissue paper and his box. "I was talking to the Lamb and the Clown only last night. Well, it will not be so bad if I can see them once in a while. I should also like to meet the Wax Doll again, and the Elephant. I hope nice fat boys get them for presents."

Though it was cold outside of Mr. Mugg's store, the Plush Bear did not feel it. In the first place, he had on his own warm coat, which was almost like fur. Then he was wrapped in paper, and he was in a box, and he was inside the nice automobile. So he was even more comfortable than he had been at the North Pole, and ever so much more cozy than when he was in the igloo of Ski, the Eskimo boy.

"Look, Nettie! Look what I have!" cried Arthur, the fat boy, as he ran into the house as soon as the auto stopped. "I have a Bear that growls!"

Nettie, his little sister, who was running to meet her brother, carrying in her arms a Rag Doll, stopped when Arthur began to open the bundle he had carried from Mr. Mugg's store.

"I don't like growly bears!" she exclaimed.

"Oh, this bear is nice! He's a Plush Bear," Arthur said. "He wobbles his head and he jiggles his paws, and he growls, but it's only a make-believe growl. Look at my new Bear, Nettie!"

Arthur quickly took the wrappings from the Plush Bear and wound up the spring as Mr. Mugg had shown him. Then, when the Bear was set down on the floor, the toy began to wave his paws, to shake his head from side to side, and from his red mouth came several growls.

"Oh! Oh!" exclaimed Nettie, who had knelt down beside her brother to look at the Bear. "I don't like him when he growls!"

"Oh, he won't hurt you, Nettie!" laughed the fat boy Arthur. "See, he's waving his paw to you, and he only growls like your rubber doll squeaks. My Plush Bear is nice, Nettie."

And when the little girl found that the Bear did no harm, but only growled in a make-believe, jolly fashion, she decided to make friends with him. She sat down on the floor close beside him, and when the clockwork inside the toy had run down, and the Bear was still, Nettie took him up in her arms and loved him.

"Isn't he nice?" asked Arthur.

"Yes, pretty nice," agreed Nettie. "But he isn't as nice as my Rag Doll."

"Well, girls like dolls and boys like Plush Bears. That's the best way, I guess," said Arthur.

Then he and his sister played some more with the Plush Bear, winding him up, listening to his pretended growls, and watching him wave his paws and shake his head.

That night after the children had gone to bed and the Plush Bear was in the closet of the playroom with the Rag Doll, the Bear leaned over and whispered to the Doll:

"What sort of place is it here?"

"Oh, very nice!" the Rag Doll answered. "Two better children than Nettie and Arthur you could not wish for! And every Summer they go to the seashore."

"The seashore? Where is that?" asked the Plush Bear. "Is it near the North Pole?"

"Oh, my, no!" answered the Rag Doll. "It is so long since I was at the North Pole, where I once lived in the shop of Santa Claus, that I have almost forgotten about it. But the seashore is quite different. I have been there with Nettie for two summers. And, now that you belong to Arthur, I suppose he will take you there. It is very jolly down on the warm sand near the sparkling waves."

"I should very much like to see it," said the Plush Bear.

There were other toys in the closet, and they talked and had a good time together that night when Arthur and Nettie were fast asleep.

And then began a happy life for the Plush Bear. The Christmas season came and went, and Nettie and Arthur received other toys, but none that they cared for any more than they did for the Rag Doll and the Plush Bear. During the Winter days and evenings other boys and girls came over to play with Arthur and Nettie, bringing their toys. In this way the Plush Bear again met the Lamb on Wheels and the Calico Clown, each of whom had been made as good as new by Mr. Mugg.

At last the warm days of Summer came, and the Rowe family started in a train for the seashore. Nettie had her Rag Doll, and Arthur carried his Plush Bear. The children had seats near the window in the train, and Arthur held his Bear up to look out. It was a warm day and the window was open.

"Be careful, Arthur!" called his mother. "Don't put your head out!"

"I won't," the fat boy promised. But he did hold his Plush Bear part way out of the window. "I want to let him see things," said Arthur.

Suddenly the train slowed up, and so quickly that the Plush Bear was jerked from the fat boy's hand. Out of the car window fell the Plush Bear!

Down, down, down out of the window of the moving train fell the Plush Bear! He heard Arthur cry as his toy was jerked from his hands, and the toy had a strange feeling inside him as he turned over and over in his plunge.

"Talk about somersaults!" thought Mr. Bruin as he sailed downward. "The Polar Bear should see me now! I wonder what is going to happen to me! I have turned more somersaults in a minute than he turned in a whole evening at the North Pole!"

"Arthur! Arthur! what is the matter?" called the fat boy's mother, when she heard him cry.

"Oh, Mother! my Plush Bear has fallen out of the window!" Arthur answered. "I was showing him the sights, and the train jiggled him out of my hand!"

"And my Rag Doll almost went out of my window, but I held on to her," added Nettie.

"Oh, you have lost your nice new Plush Bear!" exclaimed Mrs. Rowe. "I wonder if we can get him back?"

"I fancy so," said Mr. Rowe, who was taking his family to the seashore. "The train is going to stop at this station, and I can run back and pick up Arthur's toy."

The fat boy felt better when he heard his father say this, but still he was afraid lest perhaps his plaything might have been broken in the tumble.

It was the sudden slowing of the train for the station stop that had caused Arthur to drop his Plush Bear. With a grinding of the brakes the cars came to a standstill, and Mr. Rowe, followed by Arthur, started for the door. Nettie also got down out of her seat.

"No, dear, you had better stay with me," her mother said. "Daddy will get the Plush Bear back if it can be found."

"Where you s'pose he is?" asked the little girl.

And now we must find that out ourselves.

Down! down! down! turning somersault after somersault, the Plush Bear fell. Arthur had held the toy up to the window just as the train was crossing a high bridge, beneath which ran a street. The railroad tracks were on an embankment, and in the street below trees were growing. The train ran over the bridge, or trestle, above the trees.

And it was into one of these trees, growing down in the street, that the Plush Bear fell. Right down among the branches he plunged, but as it was now Summer, and there were leaves on the trees, it was almost like falling on a soft sofa cushion.

"I'm glad this tree was here!" thought the Plush Bear, as he landed on a branch among the soft leaves. "If I had struck on the hard street or on the sidewalk there is no telling what would have happened. I don't believe I'm at all hurt now."

And indeed he was not. Aside from being shaken up and having his plush ruffled, the Bear was not in the least harmed. But had he landed on the road one of his springs inside or some of his wheels might have been broken or twisted, and he never could have growled again or moved his head or paws. That is, unless Mr. Mugg could have mended him.

As it was, the Plush Bear fell down into the tree, and there he stuck on a branch not far from the ground. The Plush Bear sat astraddle the limb.

"Oh, I am not safe yet!" he thought. "Maybe I'll fall after all! I must keep very still and quiet until I see what will happen next."

By this time the train had stopped and Arthur and his father were alighting at the small station.

"This isn't where you get off," said the conductor to Mr. Rowe. "This isn't the seashore."

"I know it," said Mr. Rowe. "But my little boy dropped his Plush Bear out of the window, and we're going back to see if we can get it. Have we time?"

"Yes," answered the conductor. "The train has to wait here five minutes to have some trunks taken off. But don't be too long. I hope you may find the little boy's toy."

Arthur hoped so himself, as he hurried down to the street level.

"Where do you think my Bear is, Daddy?" he asked.

"It must be somewhere near the bridge," was the answer. "I heard you call out as the train rumbled over it."

Along the street which ran near the railroad walked Arthur and his father. As they walked they looked carefully on the ground for sight of the Plush Bear, but he was not to be found.

"I'm sure you must have dropped him about here," said Mr. Rowe, as he and the fat boy stood beneath the railroad bridge. "But he isn't in sight. Perhaps some one picked him up."

"Oh, is my nice Plush Bear gone?" sighed Arthur.

He looked all around, but Mr. Bruin, as the Bear was sometimes called, was not in sight. Then a ragged little boy, who had been flying a kite, came running along the street.

"What's the matter?" asked the ragged lad. "Did you lose your ball?"

"No; it's my Plush Bear," answered Arthur. "I dropped him out of the car window, but I don't see him now."

The ragged boy looked up into the tree under which he and the fat boy and Mr. Rowe were standing. There, right over their heads, stretched out on a limb to which he seemed to be clinging with all four paws, was the Plush Bear. The toy had been looking down at Arthur and his father, and he had been wishing he might call and tell them where he was, but of course this was not allowed.

"I see him! I'll get him for you!" cried the ragged boy.

In another moment he was climbing the tree, and a little later he tossed down the Plush Bear, Mr. Rowe catching the toy in his hands.

"Now I have him back again! Oh, I'm so glad! Now I have my Plush Bear!" cried Arthur. "I'll never let you fall out of a window again!"

"I should hope not!" said Mr. Rowe, as he gave his fat son the toy. "And here is twenty-five cents for you, little man," he added to the ragged boy.

"Oh, thanks!" cried the barefoot lad, as he ran away down the street, the shining silver quarter held tightly in his hand. Then Arthur and his father went back to their train, the fat boy holding the Plush Bear in his arms.

"Oh, you found him! I'm so glad!" said Mrs. Rowe, as her husband and son took their seats and the train started. "You must be careful after this, Arthur."

"I will," promised the little boy.

"And I'm going to be careful of my Rag Doll," said Nettie, as she held her plaything on her lap.

There were no more accidents during the trip to the seashore, which was reached in the afternoon. Mr. and Mrs. Rowe went to the hotel with their son and daughter, and of course the Plush Bear and the Rag Doll went also.

"Where is this ocean you talked about?" asked the Plush Bear of the Rag Doll when they had a moment alone together.

"Oh, it is outside. Did you think they kept the ocean in the hotel?" asked the Doll, with a laugh.

"I didn't know," the Bear remarked. "Is this a hotel?"

"Yes; it's a great big house where the family lives while at the seashore," the Doll said. "You'll like it here. This is my third summer, and I—"

But just then the door opened and Arthur and Nettie came running into the room. Of course the toys could no longer talk to each other.

"We're going down on the boardwalk in wheeled chairs!" cried Nettie. "I'm going to take my Rag Doll."

"And I'll take my Plush Bear," said Arthur. "To-morrow I'll play with him on the sand."

"I wonder what all this means—wheeled chairs—sand—boardwalk?" thought the Plush Bear. "So many things are happening I cannot keep track of them!"

Suddenly he found himself shut up with the two children and the Rag Doll in a sort of iron cage. And, all of a sudden, it began to go down.

"Goodness! am I falling again?" thought the Plush Bear.

He looked at the Rag Doll, but she did not seem to be startled. And then he heard Nettie say:

"Don't you like to go down in the elevator, Arthur?"

"Yes, it's lots of fun," answered the fat boy.

"Oh, it seems I am in an elevator," thought the Plush Bear. "Something else new!"

He soon grew used to the motion, and a little later he and Arthur, with Nettie and her Doll, were seated in a big chair on Wheels, and were being pushed along a broad wooden walk by a colored man.

"Isn't there a big crowd on the boardwalk?" said Arthur to his sister, as they were being wheeled along.

"Yes, but not as large as this time last year," replied the little girl. "Look out, Arthur!" she suddenly cried. "Your Bear is slipping! If he falls under the wheels he'll be run over!"

Arthur made a grab for his toy, which had been resting in his lap, but he was not quick enough. Down out of the wheeled chair slipped the Plush Bear! Down to the boardwalk, and right toward him rumbled another big double chair, in which sat a fat man and a large woman.

CHAPTER VIII

IN THE SAND

Sometimes things occur very luckily in this world. If it had not happened that the colored man, who was pushing the big, double, wheeled chair, looked down at the boardwalk and saw the Plush Bear just in time, Mr. Bruin would have been crushed. His spring that made him move his head and paws and the growler inside him would have been broken to bits. But, as it happened, the colored chair-pusher saw the Plush Bear fall from the lap of Arthur Rowe, who sat beside his sister Nettie in a chair on the boardwalk at the seaside city.

"Hi! My land! Wait a minute!" shouted the colored man.

"Maybe he is going to save me!" thought the Plush Bear, who had seen the rubber-tired wheels coming nearer and nearer.

"What's the matter, Sam?" asked the man in the big rolling chair.

At the same time Arthur leaned forward with a cry of alarm, for he saw his Plush Bear had slipped, as it had slipped from him and out of the car window the day before.

"Li'l boy done drop his play-toy!" answered Sam, the colored man. "I come nigh onto runnin' ober it. Heah it is, li'l man," went on the chair-pusher as he picked up the Plush Bear and handed him back to Arthur.

"Oh, thank you!" exclaimed Arthur, while Nettie, who had seen what almost had happened, held her Rag Doll tighter in her arms.

"I'm not going to drop Polinda, not ever!" declared Nettie. Polinda was the name of her doll. When Nettie first received the toy she had wanted to call the doll Polly, but the little girl next door said Lucinda would be a better name. So Nettie mixed up both names and called her doll Polinda, which is a very good name, I think.

With his Plush Bear safe in his arms once more, Arthur leaned back in his rolling chair. He and Nettie smiled at the lady and gentleman in the chair that had almost run over Mr. Bruin, and then the two chairs were pushed on by the men rolling them. Just behind Arthur and his sister, in another chair, were Mr. and Mrs. Rowe, but they had been so busy, looking at the sights along the boardwalk, they had not seen how nearly there was an accident.

"Is your Bear all right?" asked Nettie of her brother, as they were wheeled along. "I mean will his head nod?"

"His head doesn't exactly nod," replied Arthur. "I guess you're thinking of Joe's Nodding Donkey. But my Bear wags his head."

"Maybe he won't now, after all that happened," suggested Nettie.

"Oh, I guess he will," said Arthur. "But I'll wind him up and see."

He turned the key that wound up the spring, and as soon as it was tight enough the Plush Bear began to move his paws, shake his head from side to side and growl in a gentle voice, just as Santa Claus had intended he should do.

"He's all right," said Arthur.

"Thank goodness for that!" exclaimed the Plush Bear to himself. "One never knows what may happen when one falls out of a car window and then from a wheeled chair to the boardwalk. I might have got a lot of slivers in me, or have loosened a wheel! I'm glad I'm all right."

After an hour spent on the boardwalk, seeing the many sights and looking at the waves of the ocean rolling up on the sandy beach, Arthur and his sister, with their father and mother, went back to their hotel. Evening was coming on and it was time for supper, or dinner as it is called in fashionable seaside hotels, for the principal meal is served in the evening instead of at noon.

"I wish we could go down and play on the sand," said Nettie, as she and her brother got out of the wheeled chair. "My Rag Doll wants to go barefoot on the beach."

"And I think my Plush Bear would like it, too," said Arthur.

"You may go down and play in the sand all day to-morrow," promised their mother.

"Oh, won't we have fun!" cried Nettie. "Maybe my Rag Doll can learn to swim."

"Well, swimming won't hurt her," said Arthur; "but I'm not going to let my Plush Bear get in the water. I'm going to make a sand cave for him to live in."

"Well, it seems I am to have some fun," thought the toy, as he was taken up in the elevator.

The Plush Bear did not like the elevator very much. It gave him a queer feeling among his wheels and spring; and his grunter, by means of which he growled, seemed to be turning over and over. But this did not last long, and while Arthur and Nettie, with their parents, were at dinner in the hotel, the Bear and the Doll had a chance to talk.

"How do you like it at this fashionable seaside hotel?" asked the Bear.

"Quite well," answered the Doll, lifting her eyebrows the way she had seen some ladies doing in the hotel parlor as she was carried in. "I wish Nettie would put a different dress on me, though," the Doll added. "It is fashionable to dress here in the evening, but she has left my old clothes on."

"Old clothes are best," growled the Bear. "You feel more comfortable in them. I don't need any, I'm glad to say, not even at the cold North Pole. But say, Rag Doll, now we're alone, let's do something."

"I know what we can do!" the Rag Doll exclaimed. "All my life I have wanted to play with the glistening things in a hotel bathroom. I want to work the shower, and turn the shiny handles. There are ever so many more than we have at home. Come on into the bathroom, and let's turn every handle we see!"

"All right," agreed the Plush Bear. "That'll be fun!"

And there is no telling what mischief he and the Rag Doll might have got into, only, just then, in came Nettie and Arthur, having finished dinner.

"I'm going to play with my Plush Bear!" cried the fat boy.

"And I'm going to get my Rag Doll to sleep," said Nettie. "It's time she was in bed."

The Doll and the Bear could only look slyly at one another. There was no chance now for them to have fun with the shiny handles in the bathroom. But perhaps it was just as well.

That night, when Arthur and Nettie, as well as their father and mother were asleep, the Bear and Doll had a chance to make believe come to life, move about, and speak.

"But we won't turn the handles in the bathroom and splash the water now," said the Doll. "It would make such a noise that they'd awaken and we'd be caught. But what can we do?"

"Let's look out the windows," suggested the Plush Bear. So, climbing up first on little stools, and then on chairs, the two toys looked from the hotel windows. They saw many lights sparkling, and out to sea was a tall lighthouse with a gleaming beacon which flickered like a giant lightning bug.

In the morning Arthur and Nettie went down on the sand to play, the little fat boy taking his Plush Bear and Nettie her Rag Doll.

"Oh, what a dandy Teddy Bear!" cried a small, red-haired chap as he ran along the beach to play with Arthur.

"This isn't a Teddy Bear," explained Arthur. "He's a Plush Bear, and he can move his head and his paws and he can growl."

"Let's hear him!" begged the red-haired boy.

So Arthur wound up the spring, and, surely enough, the toy did all those things.

"Oh, he's a dandy!" cried the red-haired lad. "If you let me play with him, I'll let you take my airship that flies."

"We'll take turns playing with them," said Arthur, and then began a happy time for the children. Some little girls came over to play with Nettie, and they had lots of fun on the sand.

After a while Arthur happened to think of what he had said he was going to do—dig a sand cave for his Bear.

"We'll make a big one," he said to the red-haired lad. "We'll dig a big hole."

"With clam shells!" cried the other lad, and, putting aside the Plush Bear and the airship, the two little friends began to make a large hole in the sand. When it was finished the Plush Bear was put down in it, and some sticks were stuck up in front.

"We'll make believe the sticks are the bars of his cage," said Arthur. "We'll pretend he's a circus Bear."

"Oh, yes," agreed the red-haired boy. "That's lots of fun."

So they played with the Plush Bear in the hole of the sand for some time. Then other boys and girls came along, joining in the fun, and pretty soon some children rode past on ponies.

"Oh, I'm going to ask mother if we can't ride on the ponies!" cried Nettie.

"So'm I!" added her brother, and, forgetting all about the Plush Bear in the hole, away they ran to tease for ponies to ride. Mrs. Rowe was sitting on the sand not far from where the children had been playing.

"Yes, Arthur and Nettie, you may ride the ponies," she said. "I'll take you down and tell the man to put you on."

And in the excitement of the pony ride Arthur forgot all about his Plush Bear in the sand cave. The toy was left there all alone, and he did not know what to think.

"I wonder if I dare knock down those sticks they call bars and climb out?" thought the toy. "I don't believe any one is looking." He was just going to do this when along the beach dashed one of the ponies with a little girl on his back. The pony stepped close to the hole where the Plush Bear was, and in another instant the sand caved in, covering Mr. Bruin from sight!

CHAPTER IX

OUT TO SEA

Sand ran down into the eyes of the Plush Bear. Grains of sand tickled his plush toes. Some even got in his plush mouth that he opened when he gave his growls. Other grains of sand trickled between the joints of his paws and his body.

"Oh, dear, this is terrible!" said Mr. Bruin, as he found himself in darkness when the hole into which Arthur had placed him caved in from the feet of the pony. "This is simply terrible!"

But though the Plush Bear, being by himself, was allowed to talk and move about, pretending to come to life, he soon found that it was not wise to open his mouth. The wider he opened it the more sand came in.

"What shall I do?" thought the Plush Bear to himself, not opening his mouth to say anything this time. "How am I ever going to get out of here?"

Well might he ask himself that, for the sand was so closely packed in about him that he could hardly move. Even though the spring inside him was wound up, the Plush Bear could not turn his head nor wave his paws. As for growling, he knew better than to try that.

"Well, something must be done!" thought the Plush Bear. "If I stay in this sand hole too long I'll smother! I wonder why Arthur doesn't come and take me out? He always said he was fond of me!"

But Arthur, the fat boy, was just then having a glorious ride on a pony, and Nettie, his sister, was also having a ride. For the time being the children had forgotten about their toys. Nettie had left her Rag Doll and Arthur his Plush Bear. But the Rag Doll was not buried in the sand.

Up and down along the sand rode the children on the backs of the beach ponies. But at last Mrs. Rowe decided that Nettie and Arthur had had fun enough, so she helped them out of the little saddles.

"Get your playthings and come to the hotel. We must dress for dinner," she said. "Where is your Rag Doll, Nettie? And your Plush Bear, Arthur?"

"I left my Rag Doll on the sand," answered Nettie. "I'll get her."

"And I left my Plush Bear—Oh, I left him in the sand circus cage, where I was playing he was a wild Bear!" cried Arthur. "Oh, I forgot, I left my nice Plush Bear in a hole!"

"You'd better get him out as soon as you can," said his mother.

The children remembered the spot where they had been playing on the sand before they took the pony rides. Nettie ran back there, and soon found her Rag Doll.

"But where's my Plush Bear?" asked Arthur anxiously, looking up and down the beach. "I made a hole here, right by Nettie's Doll, and I put sticks in the hole, like bars in a circus cage, and I left my Plush Bear in the hole."

"Are you sure this is the place?" asked Mrs. Rowe, as she, too, looked searchingly up and down the sand. She did not want Arthur to lose his toy.

"It was right here," declared the fat boy.

"I don't see any hole," went on Mrs. Rowe. Of course she did not know that the pony had scattered the sand, filling up the little cave Arthur had made.

"Oh, where is my Plush Bear?" cried the little fat boy, and he was almost ready to cry. His mother and Nettie helped him look. So did other children, wandering up and down the beach, but there was no sign of the toy. Then a coast guard, one of the men who march up and down the sands, keeping watch for shipwrecks, came along the boardwalk.

"Have you lost something?" asked the guard, as he came down the steps from the boardwalk to the beach.

"We lost a Bear," said Arthur.

"A bear?" cried the guard, in surprise. "A—a bear?"

"My little boy means a Plush Bear," explained Mrs. Rowe, and then she told what had happened.

"Oh, a toy, buried in the sand," said the guard, laughing. "Well, that's too bad. Right around here, was it? Well, I happened to be passing this afternoon, and I noticed just about the spot where the children were sitting on the sand. I didn't see the Plush Bear, but I know the children were digging, and it wasn't at this spot—it was nearer the ocean. Over here it was," the guard went on, moving away from the place where Ar thur had been sure he had made the cave for the toy. "You see, we coast guards get in the habit of noticing things and remembering where they are," he added. "You were looking in the wrong place. I fancy your Bear must have been covered up in some way. I'll dig here!"

With a stick the guard began digging, and in a little while he uncovered the Plush Bear.

"Oh, there he is! There he is!" cried Arthur, as he saw his toy again. "Oh, thank you for finding him for me!" and he took his plaything from the hands of the coast guard.

"Yes, that's what I say—thanks a whole lot of times!" murmured the Plush Bear to himself, as once more he was able to breathe. "This was the most terrible adventure I ever had!"

But the Plush Bear was to have one even worse, as you shall soon hear.

"You must be more careful of your toys, Arthur," said his mother, as, having thanked the man, she and her children went back to the hotel.

"I'll never put him in a sand hole again," promised the little fat boy.

That night, when Arthur and Nettie were snug in their beds, and the Plush Bear and the Rag Doll were in a closet by themselves, the Doll leaned over and said:

"Wasn't it terrible, Mr. Bear?"

"It certainly was," agreed the Plush Bear. "I'm full of grit as it is. Sand is all over me, even though Arthur did brush me off with a little broom. I seem to squeak instead of growling as I ought to."

"Oh, well, maybe you'll be better after a while," said the Rag Doll. Then she and the Plush Bear talked together in the darkness, but the Bear did not feel like playing. He was too much shocked by having been buried in the sand.

"Now we're going to have some fun, Plush Bear!" cried Arthur the next morning, as he took his toy from the closet. "We're going in swimming!"

"Swimming? Swimming?" repeated the Plush Bear to himself. "I wonder what that means?"

If he had been a real bear he would have known, for real bears, that live in the woods, are very fond of playing in the water. But, being only a Santa Claus toy, the Plush Bear knew nothing of this.

A little later Arthur and Nettie were down on the sand in their bathing suits. All along the beach were many other children and grown folk, too, in their bathing suits. Nettie carried her Rag Doll and Arthur had his Plush Bear.

"Oh, Arthur! you aren't going to take your toy into the water with you, are you?" asked his mother.

"No'm," the little fat boy answered. "I'm just going to play with him on the sand till Daddy comes to teach me to swim. And I'm not going to put my Bear in a hole, either!"

"I'm glad of that, anyhow," thought the Plush Bear, who heard all that was said. "Once in a sand hole is enough for me."

Arthur's father was going to teach the little fat boy to swim, and while waiting for Daddy, Arthur played about on the sand with the Plush Bear, as Nettie played with her Rag Doll.

Now and then Arthur, with the Plush Bear in his arms, would wade out a little way into the water, and he would laugh, and run back, as the incoming tide would send a wave over his bare toes.

"Be careful, Sonny!" called his mother, as she watched him. "The waves are getting higher and higher. I wish your father would come and give you your swimming lesson."

"Oh, I'm having fun!" laughed the fat boy. "My Plush Bear likes me to carry him out, but I won't let him fall in the ocean."

Once more the little fat boy started to wade down the beach. Nettie had gone back to sit with her mother and, for a moment, Arthur was all by himself. Except, of course, he had the Plush Bear with him.

"Look and see how big the ocean is, Mr. Bear," said Arthur, holding his toy up above the waves. And just then a bigger wave than any that had yet rolled up the beach broke right at Arthur's feet.

In an instant the big wave had knocked the little fellow down. Arthur gave a scream, and his father, who had just arrived in his bathing suit, ran to get his little boy. Arthur had let go the Plush Bear when the wave knocked him down.

Into the water fell the toy, and, a moment later, when the wave washed back into the ocean, it took Mr. Bruin with it. Right out to sea the Plush Bear was washed, on the top of the big wave!

"Oh! Oh, dear! What is going to happen to me now?" thought the poor Plush Bear.

CHAPTER X

SAVED AT LAST

When the big wave knocked Arthur down and the little fat boy dropped the Plush Bear into the sea, that toy expected he would at once sink to the bottom and be drowned. It was the first time he had ever fallen into the water. At the North Pole, where he had been made in the workshop of Santa Claus, it is so cold nearly all the time that all water is frozen into ice, and there is very little into which one may fall.

"This is the last of me!" thought the poor Plush Bear, as he felt the water closing over his head. Faintly he heard the screams of Arthur, as the waves rolled the fat boy over and over on the beach. But Arthur's father quickly sprang in and picked up his little fat son, saving him.

There was no one at hand just then to save the Plush Bear.

"Yes, this is the last of me!" thought Mr. Bruin. But, to his surprise, he found that, after his first drop into the ocean when the waters closed over his head, he bobbed up again and floated nicely like a piece of wood.

Much of what was inside the Plush Bear was sawdust and cork, making him very light, so that, though he did not know it, he was a better floater than was Arthur.

The Plush Bear had been careful not to breathe when he fell into the sea, so he did not sniff any water up his nose. And after the first shock he did not feel bad. The water was warm, and by keeping his mouth closed the Plush Bear did not taste any of the salt. There he was, floating on his back, his big, yellow eyes staring up at the sun and the blue sky. And now, as the tide had turned and was going out, the Bear was carried out to sea with it.

Back on the beach there was much excitement when Arthur's father had pulled the fat boy out of the sea. But it was soon found that Arthur was all right, except that he had swallowed a little salt water.

"But where's my Plush Bear?" Arthur cried, when he had been dried and comforted by his mother. "Where's my Plush Bear?"

Where, indeed? Well might Arthur ask that, for his Plush Bear was being carried far, far out to sea on the waves.

"Oh, Arthur! did you drop Mr. Bruin when the wave knocked you down?" asked Nettie.

"I guess—I guess I did!" answered her brother sadly.

"Then that's the last of your Plush Bear," said Arthur's father. "But don't cry!" he told the little boy. "I'll get you another. Don't cry! There is salt water enough around here without your adding to it by your tears!" he laughed. But Arthur felt too unhappy to laugh.

And all this while Mr. Bruin was floating on the waves.

"This is certainly the strangest thing that ever happened to me," thought the Plush Bear. "I thought surely my end had come when Arthur dropped me. But, though I am all wet outside, I seem to be dry inside."

On and on floated the Plush Bear; then, all of a sudden, he heard voices talking. The voices were those of men and children, and not the voices of toys.

"Don't you like it here, Joe?" asked a boy.

"Yes, I do, Herbert," was the answer. "And my Nodding Donkey likes it, too."

"My Monkey on a Stick is having fun, and he isn't seasick a bit," said the boy who had been called Herbert. "He loves to ride in a motor boat, my Monkey does."

"What's this? What's this!" thought the Plush Bear. "Nodding Donkey? Monkey on a Stick?"

He tried to raise himself in the water to look toward the place whence came the voices, but the Plush Bear could see nothing. A moment later, though, he heard one of the boys call:

"Oh, look! What's that floating in the water?"

"It's a fish!" said the other boy.

"That isn't a fish! It's some sort of floating toy," was the answer in a man's voice. "Well, I declare, it's a Teddy Bear!"

"I'm not a Teddy Bear at all," said Mr. Bruin to himself; "but if you rescue me from the water you may call me anything you wish."

The Plush Bear Meets Nodding Donkey and Monkey On a Stick.

The Plush Bear Meets Nodding Donkey and Monkey On a Stick.

A moment later, after he had been afloat for some hours, the Plush Bear felt himself being lifted from the sea, and in another second he was placed in the bottom of a motor boat. In the boat were two men and two boys, but when the water had run out of his eyes the Plush Bear was more interested in looking at two other toys which were also in the boat.

On one seat was a Nodding Donkey who seemed to be bowing in a most pleasant and jolly fashion to the Plush Bear. And on the other seat, beside a boy, was a Monkey on a Stick.

"Oh, I have heard of these toys," thought the Plush Bear. "They, too, were once in the shop of Santa Claus! Oh, how glad I am! I'm saved at last!"

"Where do you suppose this Plush Bear came from?" asked Joe, the boy who had the Nodding Donkey.

"I think he must have fallen overboard out of some boat when some children were being given a ride, just as you boys are having a ride," said the father of Herbert. Herbert, you know, owned the Monkey on a Stick.

"I wish I could keep that Plush Bear," softly said Joe. "Now that I'm not lame any more I could run around and have fun with him."

"It is a very nice Plush Bear," said Mr. Richmond, Joe's father, as he examined the wet toy. "Some little boy or girl will be glad to get it back. It doesn't seem to be much harmed." He wound up the spring and at once the Plush Bear began to move his paws, wag his head, and growl. The growl was a trifle rusty and a bit gritty from the sand still inside the works, but that did not matter.

"We'll take the Plush Bear back to shore with us," said Joe's father. "Perhaps some children stopping at one of the hotels, or even at our own hotel, may claim this toy. We must find out. I'll put the Bear on his back in the sun so he'll dry."

"And I'll put my Nodding Donkey back there, too, so Mr. Bruin won't be lonesome," offered Joe.

"Put my Monkey there, too," said Herbert.

So the three toys were placed near each other on the back seat of the boat, and then the two boys and their father gathered in the bow, or front part, to look across the ocean. They were out for a pleasure ride.

"How did you come to be floating in the sea all by yourself?" asked the Nodding Donkey in a whisper of the Plush Bear.

"A big wave knocked Arthur down and he dropped me," was the answer, in the same low voice.

The Plush Bear was just going to tell more of his adventures when the motor boat was run up alongside a dock, and the party got out.

"I'll carry the Plush Bear," said Joe's father. "He isn't quite dry yet. We'll take him to our hotel, and I'll tell the clerk to post up a notice, saying the toy was found at sea. Then whoever owns him may claim him."

But matters were not going to turn out just that way. As it happened, Joe and Herbert were stopping at the same hotel where Arthur and Nettie were with their father and mother. Joe and Herbert had just arrived that day, which was why Arthur and Nettie had not seen their little friends before.

Coming back from their boat ride, on which they had rescued at sea the Plush Bear, the two men and the two boys entered the hotel. As they walked toward the desk, Mr. Richmond carrying the Plush Bear, there was a cry of delight from a small boy who fairly leaped out of a big, easy chair.

"There's my Plush Bear! There's my Plush Bear!" cried Arthur, for it was he. "Oh, where did you get him?" he cried, as he looked at the damp toy in Mr. Richmond's hand.

"Is this your toy?" asked Joe's father.

"Oh, yes, that's my Mr. Bruin!" cried Arthur. "I dropped him in the ocean when a big wave knocked me down, and I thought he was drowned. Oh, where'd you get him?"

"He was floating on a wave, and we saw him from our motor boat," explained Joe. And then Herbert, with his Monkey on a Stick, stepped forward, and Nettie came out of her chair, and the children were soon all together, laughing with each other in the hotel parlor.

Arthur wound up his toy, which seemed to work as well as ever, though it was still damp.

"Now we can have lovely fun!" said Nettie, when the story of the rescue of Mr. Bruin had been told by those who were in the boat. "I can play with my Rag Doll, Herbert can make his Monkey do funny tricks, the Donkey will nod his head and Arthur's Bear will growl."

And so the children played in the hotel with their toys, while their fathers and mothers talked together.

"That Plush Bear has had many adventures," said Mrs. Rowe to Joe's mother. "He fell out of a car window, he was buried in the sand, and he was carried out to sea." Of course she knew nothing of the time he had spent in the ice igloo of the little Eskimo boy.

"Yes," said Mrs. Richmond, "Joe's Donkey had many adventures, also."

"And so did Herbert's Monkey," said that little boy's mother.

"Adventures! I should say so!" exclaimed the Plush Bear to the Donkey and Monkey, when they were alone for a moment. "But I never want to fall into the ocean again!"

And he never did, I am glad to say. I wish I might tell you more of the adventures of the Monkey, the Donkey, the China Cat and Plush Bear. But this book is quite filled, as you may see. Though of course I may write other books about other toys if you think you would like them. But now we must say good-by to the Plush Bear.

THE END